*May the true [...]
your own memories [...]
be at the forefront of your [...]
I hope A Dollar a Piece inspires [...]
you to pick up a used book and
dream of it's previous owners.
Happy Reading!*

A Dollar a Piece

Dawn A. Fuller

Lady Blue Publishing

First Printing, 2017
ISBN 978-1-548-25737-8

Lady Blue Publishing
www.ladybluepublishing.com

Designed by Heather L. Nonnemacher
Edited by Alaina Richardson

For K. Rest with the angels now.

A Dollar a Piece

Dawn A. Fuller

Martin determined many years ago that he could quite happily spend the rest of his days discovering invaluable, rare treasures in the middle of absolutely nowhere for mere pennies.

The only treasures worth having were books.

Old books. Paperbacks. Hard copies. Out-of-print books. Signed books. Limited editions. First editions. First UK editions.

Disneyland, bah! According to Martin, the happiest place on earth was a poorly-marked bookstore that smelled of yellowing pages covered with sweet vanilla ink. Where it was didn't really matter much. How could there be any place better in this world than a rundown used bookstore? Exotic, sunny locales offering frosty, fruit-filled drinks; fancy, black-tie-only restaurants that serve too-small portions; candlelit beachside cafes on balmy summer nights—you can keep 'em. Any day of the week could be made better simply by visiting an independent used bookstore.

Martin spent many tedious hours updating his hand-drawn map—pinpointing his favorite used bookstores on the dusty outskirts of remote desert areas. He was *positive* no one but him knew that these book "hot spots" existed. They couldn't. Otherwise, the grabby pigs would be flocking to them at all hours of the day and night. The line would be out the door. The greedy guts would buy them all up. There would be no books left. The world as he knew it would cease to exist. Martin worried about this very thing from time to time.

Martin spent most weeknights watching *Jeopardy*, updating his book notecards, organizing his endless bookshelves, and re-reading his favorite books—reading copies only, of course. He dare not sully a rare edition by opening a book too far and making an accidental crease, or leaving a sugar-coated fingerprint on a pristine page.

Martin carefully planned his weekend shopping route in the order of where he found his most recent treasure, and by which bookseller he liked most, or least. There were only a handful of "mosts," and the last two booksellers he liked least were both dead now.

In Martin's mind, three kinds of booksellers existed: There were old, distinguished men who loved books and authors better than anything else. They knew everything there was to know. These booksellers were like walking and talking wooden card catalogues from the old brick library down the street from Martin's childhood home. Then, there were retired old fools with too much free time on their hands and the *novel* thought of a "sweet little book nook" for friends and family to "come 'round for a 'cuppa tea and a chat" in their golden years. These simple dunderheads had no idea what they actually had and couldn't care less. Such people didn't *deserve* to own a bookstore. Finally, there were selfish, obsessive hoarders who would rather die a scurrilous death than part with even *one* book out of thousands, for any price.

Saturday afternoons, Martin roamed aisle after aisle in the grainy, cool catacombs of sleepy, used bookstores. Sometimes, a random ray of warm sunlight shone through the smudged and scratched store windows. At just the right angle, a sunny laser beam chocked-full of hurling dust motes pointed straight at a beautiful used book. Martin inhaled deeply. He breathed in all that was good about books. It was times like these that Martin felt like he was the last man on earth, captured by a spiky, iron-clad, Mad-Max-like overlord—with loads of gel in his standy-upy hair—who set before him a do-or-die scavenger hunt for rare or missing books in order to keep his *very life*. Martin was always up to the challenge.

On this particular Saturday, Martin went to his favorite bookstore, *Last Chance*, located on the lonely, forsaken edge of Palm Desert. The bookseller at *Last Chance* was of the third hoarding-and-non-selling variety. From the looks of it, the bookseller's brain was just as chaotic as her overflowing, disorganized piles that hardly left enough room for a stick figure to walk between. Martin thought the bookseller herself was like many of the books *Last Chance* offered—a worthless ex-library book no one would ever want masquerading as a signed first edition of

To Kill a Mockingbird. Shiver. Horrible.

Secretly, Martin got an exhilarating thrill out of haggling with *Last Chance*'s bookseller over the crappy books she had to offer. Her absolutely *outrageous* prices for something as detestable as a ruffled *Goosebumps* paperback with scribbled-up and torn-out pages made Martin's blood boil. It also made him "tisk-tisk" aloud.

Martin always approached the cluttered *Last Chance* counter, where he could barely make out the messy head of the bookseller behind enormous, ancient piles of *National Geographic*, with the same strategy—snottily explaining why the price of a particular book was beyond ridiculous by illuminating the poor book quality and *obvious* flaws. He pointed out that the book would surely sit on the bookseller's disintegrating shelves for years and years until the entire bookshop collapsed around her. Martin would offer her what was—in his humble opinion—an undeniably *fair* price for its worth. It was then the bookseller's turn to bark, "No!"

Martin kept rubber-banded 4x4 index cards covered with his spidery scrawl in his shirt pocket at all times. On the faded cards, he kept detailed running lists of books he needed to complete a series, books he wanted to find a second readers' copy for, or rare books that no one in the world seemed to have. Each time Martin found a missing book for his collection, he concealed his excitement by purposely displaying the same sour face he made when he was served gulyás by his angry Hungarian ex-wife, Margaréta. On the inside, Martin was doing the gleeful Snoopy dance from *Charlie Brown*. He had perfected the act.

This particular Saturday, Martin could hardly believe his eyes when he saw it.

A SIGNED FIRST EDITION OF *HEARTS IN ATLANTIS*
(Signed by the Master himself, Stephen King)

Martin imagined that his euphoric brainwaves would be off the charts if tested by Johns Hopkins neurologists at this very moment. He gently patted *Hearts in Atlantis* several times with great affection as he would an unruly pet that finally did as he was told. Martin made a perfect red checkmark on his index card.

The stars were surely shining down on Martin. As quietly as he could so he wouldn't seem weird, Martin sang both Maria *and* the Captain's parts in "Something Good" from *The Sound of Music*. He liked living life on the edge. He was good at it.

Martin left *Last Chance* carefully clutching his nubby cloth sack that read "Dance is My Bag" tightly to his chest while fighting the urge to click his feet together three times. This magical find was cause for grand celebration, and only a heartburn-inducing chili size with a large side of extra cheesy fries at Pappy & Harriet's fine eatery would do.

When he arrived home, stuffed and content from his feast, Martin set his pirate's booty carefully down atop the growing pile of unfolded clean clothes on the Barcalounger. He stuck his stolen Denny's mug from his wilder college years in the microwave for a quick reheat of his cold coffee. He thoughtfully shelved *Hearts in Atlantis* between *Gerald's Game* and *Insomnia* on the "K" bookcase. Every book had its place.

Martin took a loud slurp of his stale coffee, turned on *Jeopardy*, redeposited the heaping laundry pile onto the sofa, and half listened to Alex Trebek. Smiling, Martin glanced over at *Hearts in Atlantis*. He could barely stand to look in the general direction for fear he might rip the book off the shelf and start crying all over its pages.

"This time, with about eighteen thousand dollars in cash as well as those two Daily Doubles, here are the six categories you can choose from: National Landmarks, The 60s, Mythology, Literary Facts, Royalty, and Foreign Cuisine," said Alex Trebek, taunting Martin.

"Literary Facts for 500, Alex," Martin muttered while trying to avert his eyes from the bookshelf.

"The so-called 'hub of commerce' in Steinbeck's *Cannery Row*," said Alex Trebek.

"Mere child's play, Alex. What is Lee Chong's General Store?" Martin said blithely as he looked over again at *Hearts in Atlantis*. The suspense was killing him. He couldn't take it another second.

Martin rubbed his hands on his shirt, and even though he was alone and no one was watching, tiptoed over to the bookshelf. He fingered the spine of *Hearts in Atlantis* and stood thoughtfully for a long moment. He re-shelved part of his Terry Pratchett series in the "P" bookcase, sat back down again, and put his feet up.

"Thank you, ladies and gentlemen, for tuning in today. Until next time, I'm Alex Trebek, and I hope to see you soon on *Jeopardy!*"

Fifteen minutes later, Martin felt himself in a trance, staring at *Hearts in Atlantis* again. That was it. He couldn't bring himself to read the inscription. He knew the book was much more valuable with King's autograph, which was part of its allure. However, Martin also viewed the author's personal messages to other readers like he did new lovers insisting on disclosing their sexual history straight away just because they wanted to hear yours—damaging, to say the least. He didn't want to know there was anyone before *him*. Martin wanted to be *The One*. He refused to think about it—ever. His women didn't have histories—neither did his books. Unbearable. It was only him, now and always.

Martin turned to page six.

"Bobby looked at him in fascination, his empty belly temporarily forgotten. He loved the idea of time as an old bald cheater—it was absolutely and completely right, although he couldn't have said why . . . and didn't that very inability to say why somehow add to the coolness? It was like a thing inside an egg, or a shadow behind pebbled glass.

'Who's Ben Jonson?'

'An Englishman, dead these many years,' Mr Brautigan said."

"Too true. Time *is* an old bald cheater. Too true," Martin said as he tenderly set the book down on the floor next to him, folded his hands behind his head, and dozed off, dreaming of undiscovered desert bookstores on lunar landscapes.

***

My Uncle Richard is dead.

The coroner said he had a pulmonary embolism. He was dead in his bed for a week before anyone found him.

Uncle Richard didn't have friends. Well, he had one friend—Desmond. Dez told the cops Uncle Richard had been sick with a bad head cold. When Uncle Richard didn't call Dez back after a few days, Dez called the cops. That was when they found Uncle Richard upstairs in his bed. Dead.

I only knew Uncle Richard when I was small. I haven't seen him in years. I can remember a car ride to the mechanic with my dad and Uncle Richard when I was a kid. Uncle Richard bought me a big vanilla ice cream with rainbow sprinkles in an extra-crunchy waffle cone with a fat cherry on top while we waited.

I wanted chocolate. I hate vanilla.

Dad said if I cleaned out Uncle Richard's house, I could do whatever I wanted with his stuff—make a buck or two. Dad couldn't deal with Uncle Richard's crap. There is a lot to do, but the kids want some new Xbox games and there are a few dresses I want at Forever 21. I should go to Vegas. I haven't been there in a long time. I need a vacation. I want to see the white tigers and Celine Dion. The welfare check is already spent. I deserve to treat myself.

The cops and the coroner's office gave me and dad the "all clear" to go into Uncle Richard's house two weeks after they found him. Dad came with me on the first day. There was still sticky yellow caution tape blocking Uncle Richard's peeling front door. Uncle Richard's old neighbors came out to stare at us when we cut the tape and went inside. Nosy bastards.

As soon as we walked in, all I saw were books. Bookcase after bookcase. Walls and walls of books. What a loser Uncle Richard was. He probably had books instead of friends or a wife and kids. How sad for someone to spend all their time reading instead of living life. What a waste. I don't have time for reading. I live *my* life.

I really didn't want to go upstairs where Uncle Richard had been lying dead in his bed. Who knew what it would look like. It would probably stink like dead people. Eventually, we had to. I bet there were just more books.

It looked like the cops had crumpled up Uncle Richard's sheets in a dirty ball and threw them on top of the bed where they found his rotting body. Dad was holding his chest like he couldn't breathe when he looked around the lifeless room with the ugly peach walls. Uncle Richard had painted his room peach. Men don't like *peach*.

Uncle Richard's closet door was open. Inside were four pairs of New Balance trainers, two sets of black dress shoes, some giant-size shirts big enough to be dresses on me, a navy-blue suit, and a tie rack with tons of brightly-colored ties hanging in a perfect row, *Sleeping with the Enemy* style. I wonder why Uncle Richard had so many ties. What did he do, put on a tie when he was at home eating piles of food and reading one of his thousands of books? Uncle Richard never went anywhere that he needed to wear a tie.

I walked over to Uncle Richard's nightstand to look at a gold picture frame. There was a picture of Uncle Richard sitting in a red leather chair wearing the navy-blue suit from the closet and one of the crazy ties. Standing behind him was a much younger girl with long blonde hair and brown eyes. Her arms were hung over his shoulders—hugging him—and her head was tilted next to his. They were both smiling. They looked happy. I can't remember Uncle Richard ever being happy.

Dad was sitting on the edge of the bed with his face in his hands. I put the gold picture frame under his face. He didn't say anything. After seeing the picture of Uncle Richard and the girl, he had to go outside for air and a smoke. This whole thing messed him up.

I really had to push up hard on Uncle Richard's bedroom window to get it open. I heard wood crack when I did. It may be stuck like that for good now. It doesn't matter. Before I went back downstairs, I picked up a gold pocket watch and a bunch of holiday cards that were stacked next to the picture frame of Uncle Richard and the girl.

Dad must have smoked a million cigarettes. He was outside forever. When he finally came back in, I asked him who the girl with Uncle Richard was. He rubbed his face. He picked a piece of tobacco off his tongue, spit, and said, "That was his girlfriend. I think they split up."

Uncle Richard probably weighed 400 pounds. He was 61 when he died. Dad said he was a total loner. Always grumpy. He had turned into one of those mental people that can't leave the house for anything. I forget what you call it. Starts with an "A." Agora-something. Uncle Richard didn't even go to the store to buy his own food. He ordered it online and had it delivered. Too lazy. I bet he ordered a bunch of bad crap. Dad said all he ever did was look up music on his computer, bet on soccer teams online, and read his boring books.

A girlfriend. Amazing.

Dad couldn't take it anymore. He went to 7-Eleven to pick up a 24-pack of Keystone and head over to Uncle Jake's to drink away Uncle Richard. Before he left, he told me to lock up when I was done for the day, and if I found any cash lying around, let him know.

It creeped me out to be in Uncle Richard's house in the first place—being alone made it even creepier.

I looked through Uncle Richard's desk and found a ton of credit card bills, restaurant take-out receipts, and more cards. I sat down on the sofa with the gold pocket watch from the nightstand and a stack of the cards. The pocket watch was shiny and looked expensive. I bit it. I think that's what you're supposed to do if you want to find out if something is real gold or fool's gold. It felt like 14 karats to me. I opened it. It was engraved.

"*Time is an old bald cheater. Love for all time, Ann.*"

Whatever *that* means.

I opened a few cards next.

"*Happy Valentine's Day to My Sweet. I can't wait to see you. You mean everything to me. You are loved and cherished. I miss you like mad. Love Always, Ann.*"

"*Merry Christmas Sweetheart. YOU are the best Christmas present of ALL. It won't be long until we are together again. I hope you cook something nice for yourself and raise a glass to us since we are apart this holiday. I will be thinking of you. Counting the days… Love Always, Ann.*"

In one card, the girl wrote a poem.

*I don't love you as if you were the salt-rose, topaz
or arrow of carnations that propagate fire:
I love you as certain dark things are loved,
secretly, between the shadow and the soul.
I love you as the plant that doesn't bloom and carries
hidden within itself the light of those flowers,
and thanks to your love, darkly in my body
lives the dense fragrance that rises from the earth.
I love you without knowing how, or when, or from where,*

I love you simply, without problems or pride:
I love you in this way because I don't know any other way of loving
but this, in which there is no I or you,
so intimate that your hand upon my chest is my hand,
so intimate that when I fall asleep it is your eyes that close.

—Pablo Neruda, Sonnet XVII

I hate poetry. It is boring and never about anything important.

Huh. Seemed like this "Ann" really had a thing for Uncle Richard. Hard to believe. I wondered if Dad and Uncle Jake ever met her. I wondered where she lived. Since Uncle Richard never went out, how had they met? Internet maybe. Ann probably thought Uncle Richard had money.

I smoked a cigarette in the kitchen and ran water over it in the sink when I was done. I went back to Uncle Richard's desk. I was sure he kept his cash in there somewhere. In the top drawer, there was a sealed envelope on its own. I opened it.

Last Will and Testament of Richard J. Attison

In the event of my death, I, Richard J. Attison, of 1220 Kent Place, Yreka, California 96097, being of sound body and mind, wish to leave my entire estate to Ms. Ann Elise Barsodi, my sole beneficiary.

I revoke all prior wills and codicils.

I give my entire interest in the real property which was my residence at the time of my death, together with any and all monies to include: life insurance, automobiles, pension earnings, investments, and any and all personal property contained in my home or elsewhere, to Ms. Ann Elise Barsodi. Ms. Ann Elise Barsodi and only Ann Elise Barsodi is to be executor of this will.

I have intentionally omitted making provisions for any immediate or distant family members who are not mentioned herein including: Dave Attison

10

(brother), Jake Attison (brother), Katie Attison (sole niece), or any other living blood relative. I generally and specifically disinherit any and all persons (each and every member of my family) who claim to lawfully be entitled to my heirs apart from Ann Elise Barsodi, my sole heir. To any such persons (family members or anyone else) who should try and contest this will, or are in any way successful in contesting my express wishes, I hereby provide the amount of one dollar ($1).

In the event of my death, immediately contact:

Ms. Ann Elise Barsodi
224 Shell Beach Road
Shell Beach, California 93448

Email: aebarsodi@gmail.com

Executed on this day of May 8, 2015

Seeing as how Uncle Richard never left the house, I would have bet money he never took this letter to an attorney. I had no doubt he just wrote it and chucked in his desk drawer. *Hmmm. Maybe not,* I thought. This meant more work for me.

I set two logs in the fireplace. I crumpled up the will's pages into tight balls and shoved them between the logs. I lit a cigarette, lit the final page, tossed it into the fireplace, and watched it burn—first red, then blue, then black.

I flicked my cigarette over the fire and looked at the biggest bookcase. I ran my fingers over some of the books, knocking some down as I did. Who cares. They all looked the same anyhow—dusty, big, boring, and with too many words. I saw a book that said "Hearts in Atlantis." I pulled it out, then shoved it back in again. Dust flew up my nose.

I had to go to three bars before I found Dad and Uncle Jake. Just to cover my bases, I told them about all of Uncle Richard's crap, and about the fake will I found.

I told Dad that the will had instructions for contacting "Ann," and about her getting everything. We all knew she didn't deserve any of it. Dad said, "If you want the money, take care of it."

We didn't know Ann. She was a nobody.

"But still," Dad said as he took a long pull off his cloudy glass of Jack. He coughed a heavy, uncontrolled smoker's cough, lost his balance on his bar stool, and nearly fell to the floor. With his busted hand from last week's fight, Uncle Jake grabbed him up.

I *would* take care of it.

Nobody needed Ann finding out on her own that Uncle Richard had died—just in case she knew about the will. No one needed her poking around about Uncle Richard's house, car, money, or anything else.

Dad and Uncle Jake scraped up the money to get Uncle Richard cremated. Doesn't seem like burning up a fat guy should cost that much to me. I wonder where we should throw the ashes. None of us wants to keep them—that's for sure.

The next few days were hell cleaning out Uncle Richard's house. He could have started a goddamn library graveyard with all the books he had. I guess Uncle Richard must have fancied himself some sort of poet. I found poems he wrote all over the place. I couldn't even read more than two without getting a massive headache.

I also found what some might call "art." There were stacks of portfolios leaned up against the cobwebby wall in the spare room with swirly pictures on them. A lot of them had dark-skinned people playing twisty horns and shiny trumpets. Jazz stuff, I suppose. It couldn't have been hip-hop because Uncle Richard was too old. Maybe they were Motown people. Who knows. Since Uncle Jake's truck was up and running again (just barely), I hauled everything to the dump. I kept what I thought I could get some cash for. It only took four trips.

I never knew you could sell so many things on Facebook. Man, you can sell just about anything. I joined as many *Books for Sale* groups as I could. I was going to make some money on these books for sure. I wouldn't have paid a dollar for any of them myself.

I stacked the books in my living room and sorted them by author. I only did this because judging from what I saw on the *Books for Sale* groups, people seemed to care about it. They were looking for one or two books by a certain author, or "collections." People paid more money for collections and I wanted to get rid of as many as I could in one go. I didn't want to add more shit to my living room. My ad for Facebook and Craigslist said, "A Dollar a Piece," with a picture of each stack next to a sign that the kids wrote with their markers saying, "Pick-up Only."

In case you can't tell, Uncle Richard's house was pretty much a dump. Dad said he would help me with listing it. I could probably make about eighty thousand dollars after I paid off all his damn credit cards. *Or,* I started thinking, *maybe I could rent it.* I sold his car on Craigslist for two thousand dollars. So far, I think I sold about half of his books.

Some weird lady that owns a bookstore has been over a couple of times. She *and* her car look NUTS. It is loaded to the top with books and other crap. It looks like she lives in it. She got a spooky look in her eyes when I told her all the books were a dollar. The first stack she went to was the one with that book *Hearts in Atlantis.* When she saw it, she practically threw her money in my face. When I looked out the window, I saw her standing by her car smiling real creepy-like and staring at the book for a long time.

She must be a crazy just like Uncle Richard.

My mom better not catch wind of any of this. She might hear

about Uncle Richard dying and somehow get it in her mind there is something in it for her. I don't know how, but she might. Just when I think she is so drugged-up that she can't remember anything, she does. She may magically come off a binge and start calling or coming over. She will do anything she can to get her hands on some cash or her next fix. She is super screwed-up.

One of the damn kids broke the gold pocket watch. When they got home from school, I was sleeping. They were messing around with the boxes in the living room. I can't leave them alone for a minute. I swear to God. I can still sell it for the gold though. I have to remember to go down to the Section Eight office tomorrow first thing.

I am almost done with everything. I emailed Ann today.

Dear Ann,

I know you don't know me, but my name is Katie. I am Richard Attison's niece, his brother Dave's daughter. I am sorry to be sending you this news in an email, but my Uncle Richard is dead. Oh Ann, it has been just awful for all of us. He died in his house, all alone, without anyone he loved around to comfort him. He had what they call a pulmonary embolism. Some kind of a clot. We heard he was sick for a while, and when we checked to see if he needed us to bring him anything, he said he was fine!

We miss him so much. I just had to tell you because I know you meant a lot to him. You were his soulmate, Ann, and he was so lucky to have you. We are all thankful you were in his life.

We are planning a really big, beautiful funeral to honor Uncle Richard. We hired a Life Celebrant. She came out to the house today. She stayed for two hours. She was great. I told her all about you and Uncle Richard. She said Uncle Richard sounds like he was definitely a "Complicated Genius." I have ordered special tailor-made suits for Dad and Uncle Jake from Italy so they will look good, and as many flowers as I can. Uncle Richard would want that. He loved flowers. Flowers have been arriving for days now. Would you help us plan Uncle Richard's Celebration of Life?

This has been so hard on me personally Ann. I don't know how much more I can take...

***

...and I haven't been eating or sleeping since he died. Uncle Richard's death is affecting my marriage and my kids. I might have to go to the doctor. I was going to start looking for a job, but I definitely won't be able to do that now that Uncle Richard has died. There is just so much to deal with. The hardest part of all, Ann, is that he didn't even leave a will. I feel so bad that I can't give you anything to remember him by. I could just cry when I think about how much you meant to him.

There is one thing. In a lot of the photos of you and Uncle Richard, I see him wearing a Raider's jacket. That must have cost a lot because my Uncle was so big. I didn't think they made jackets like that in his size. I want you to have it Ann, I really do. As soon as I stop crying, I am going to put the jacket in a box and mail it to you.

I wish I could talk to you, but I just can't. We are all too sad to talk right now, but if you have any questions, email me, and I will answer what I can.

XOXO,
Katie, Richard's Niece

***

Ann clutched her stomach with both hands and retched the contents of her bento box lunch uncontrollably over the kitchen sink until her throat burned red and her legs went wobbly. She sank to the floor in exhaustion. She read the email over and over. She sobbed into her chest, hunched in front of the computer like a stained paper napkin trampled on the ground at the end of a sunny family reunion until the suffocating, dark night closed in around her.

Ann sat motionless for hours, staring at the computer screen in numb shock. She picked up the phone and dialed her mom.

15

"You *knew* this day was coming honey. Look how he *lived*. I am so sorry," her mom said quietly.

That night in bed, Ann raged. How *dare* he. All of the lies. Eight years. EIGHT YEARS. Dead. For a week. Alone. Goddamn him.

Ann's greatest fear had been realized. How many times had she expressed her fear of him dying alone in that house? She had begged and pleaded with him time after time to take care of himself.

Instead of riding gallantly into Ann's life on a white steed, Richard had pulled up in an orange delivery truck covered in exhaust dust. Ann's failed relationships were old, and the internet was new. *Yahoo Personals* was the perfect vehicle to meet people you wouldn't otherwise encounter. It was also the perfect way to disguise your true self for lengthy periods of time by exhaling flowers that morphed into delicious words on a stranger's computer screen. When Richard had finally removed the mask, it had been too late. He had played Lancelot's lead in too many of Ann's daydreams. Reality was overrated anyway.

After the break-up, Ann and Richard had remained cautious friends, at least from Ann's perspective—long distance. She had checked on him regularly at first. Each call had ended like the last— Richard pleading for her to come back, then changing tack to shouting angry accusations in uncontrolled frustration over Ann leaving him behind. Regular, loving check-ins had gone from sweet, chirpy phone calls to happy birthday email wishes to dull, tinsel-less Merry Christmas text messages. She had loved Richard, but not in the way he had wanted.

Of course he had died. It had been coming. Inevitable.

Over the last few months, Richard had stopped answering Ann's texts and emails with any regularity—sometimes for days. On the waiting days, Ann had pushed the worries out of her mind as best she could. Each time Richard did respond, Ann couldn't help but let out a big, relieved sigh, even if the reply was just a simple "I'm fine." At least he was alive.

Ann had known what "fine" meant. Fine meant Richard was slipping down the slippery slide again. Fine meant he was spending all of his time alone in that house. Fine meant he had let his weight, high blood pressure, out-of-control diabetes, and latest debilitating bouts with self-loathing and depression start to ravage his mind and body again as if he were a totally hopeless Afghan hostage locked away in a sunless, dirt-covered hole in the cracked desert floor.

Each new day brought a new heartbreaking email from Richard's niece. Katie described every grisly detail blow-by-blow—how no one knew Richard had been dead in his bed for nearly a week because he had had no friends; how the police had been forced to break down the front door only to discover Richard's stiff, blue corpse upstairs in the lonely bed; what Katie and her father had seen once inside; and all of the other macabre details that had been discovered on—or around—Richard's rotting body. The gruesome descriptions were endless and the emails relentless. Every correspondence ended with a torturous laundry list of all that Katie had to do to plan the expensive and time-consuming funeral for Richard all on her own. There was also a lot of talk about Katie having to pay "out-of-pocket" for the *Celebration of Life* extravagances Richard *deserved* in order to be sent off to eternity in *style*.

The cost of Richard's funeral was breaking Katie and her family financially. Already wearing scraps as it was, Katie's kids would have to skip getting new school clothes this year. Richard's extra-large casket had to be special-made to fit his huge body. Katie pointed out that Richard was just *too big* when he died.

Katie hired the "Life Celebrant" for fifty dollars an hour to help honor Richard properly with the *perfect* funeral. Katie promised to send Ann a written, word-for-word transcript of the funeral—compliments of the *Life Celebrant*. Katie was proud to report that without actually knowing Richard, the *Life Celebrant* would really be able to give attendees a good feel for the *Complicated Genius*. She was totally worth it—a real lifesaver. Katie would be lost without her.

Katie pleaded with Ann to help her plan the rest of the painstaking funeral details. She said Ann's thoughts on what Richard would have wanted mattered *most*. It was all becoming too much for her. Katie wanted to honor the love that Richard and Ann had shared with Ann's valuable input. She planned to use a photo she had found of Richard and Ann for the funeral program cover. She selected the costliest program paper she could find. Her uncle deserved it—*nothing but the best.*

As soon as Katie mentioned the photo, Ann's mind pulled up the exact image in the Saturday picture show of her mind. She closed her eyes tight when it appeared and called up the late-night, fall jam session and blue cigar smoke that filled their friends' airy seaside home. The deep, soulful sounds of Davis' "Autumn Leaves" bounced off the art-covered walls in the dark. Leaning, dancing couples held each other close. They whispered into the early morning hours. They vibrated in unison with velvety, brandy-filled glasses, raised index fingers, colorful Kangol hats, dark glasses, "umm hmms" and "oh yeahs."

Ann could see Richard sitting in the red leather chair with his silk tie loosened and his shiny, navy-blue suit jacket hanging off the chair's edge. She could feel her arms around Richard's neck, resting them just so, with warm brandy and warmer Miles flowing through every inch of her relaxed, swaying body, the music calming her every worry—the momentary, false sensation of life's perfection.

Ann spent the next sleepless week bent over the whirring computer, scanning old photos for the funeral—sunny road trips to Vegas, breezy beachside naps, salty Saturday margaritas with laughing friends, late nights sipping heady red wine in smoky jazz clubs. Ann sent Katie interesting tidbits about her uncle that she was unlikely to know—selections of his best poetry, snippets of his dry sense of humor, the magical twinkle in his eye, things that had amused him to no end. Ann selected several of Richard's best poems to be read and two songs to be played, including "Autumn Leaves."

As the minutes, hours, and days ticked by, the flurries of

unrelenting emails from Katie sat perched—ready to pounce—at the top of Ann's inbox, morning after morning. Ann started to avoid opening her email altogether. Mustering the strength it would take to read the latest list of crushing discoveries only left her broken.

Like the shimmery pashmina Richard's mother had draped over Ann's freckled shoulders before she died, an altogether different blanket of quiet unease settled around Ann's tired soul. Dubious drums of deception started pounding from far away in Ann's head. She felt guilty for the mere thought, but much of what Katie was saying started to strike Ann as odd.

Richard had had one friend in the entire world who had been able to stick it aside from Ann—Dez. Aside from him, who exactly was going to attend this overdone celebration of Richard's life? His brothers, of course. His niece, Katie. Maybe a co-worker or two, but Ann seriously doubted it. Richard's constant complaints about anything and everything workplace-related to anyone who would listen, persistent daily disagreements with managers and co-workers held hostage by Richard's wild mood swings, and infinite requests for time off had made him quite unpopular. Richard had been on mental disability for the last two years and had cut contact with all of them as well.

If there was one thing that Richard had been, it was consistent. He had never changed in all the years Ann had known him. There had been only a miniature handful of solid truths that remained constant.

Richard was a loving man. Richard was a brilliant writer. Richard was artistic and funny. Richard loved the sea. Richard loved jazz. Richard *hated* his family. He had been very clear about that. He hadn't been in touch with them for years. Lazy low-lives. Alcoholics. Street urchins. Especially his brother Dave's daughter, Katie. Never worked a day in her life. Begged money off everyone she could. Got pregnant at sixteen so she could to get into the system. All of them—swindlers, hustlers, grifters.

Richard's stoic refusal to attend any funeral, including that of his very own mother, made the idea of an overblown circus-like *Celebration of Life* all the more ridiculous to Ann. He would have had none of it. He would have been mortified to know his family members were even in contact with Ann, let alone planning a funeral.

No, Richard wouldn't like any of this *one bit.*

Snippets of remembered conversations popped in and out for uninvited visits, coming much too frequently and overstaying their welcome like annoying, long-lost relatives sharing inappropriate stories late into the night that no one wants to hear. Random memories—good and bad—peeked around the dark, forgotten corners of Ann's mind.

After Richard's stomach surgery and various health diagnoses, Ann had cleared all the sugar out of the house. She had scrubbed his back softly and wiped noxious sweat beads off his smooth, bald head. As he healed, they had walked around and around the shady Jacaranda-lined streets of Ann's neighborhood. His weight went down. His sugar was under control. His attitude toward life improved. Things had been looking up.

The quiet, sober ending of them was more than expected. Unavoidable. Ann couldn't move past the mammoth mountain of peculiar, needless lies. Richard was twenty years older than he had purported to be. He would secretly binge for days on soft piles of powdery donuts, cheesy platters of lasagna, and buckets of greasy fried chicken. He would spend money he didn't have with wild abandon on extravagant frivolities, leaving him over thirty thousand dollars in debt. He had acted out the tearful, drawn-out tragedy of his grandfather's death and its devastating impact on him with brightly feathered Shakespearean flair. His grandfather was alive, not dead—very much alive. Relationships ended because people were out to get *him.* Things happened *to* him. He played no role in any of it.

After promising Ann a large, loud family of their own from the day they met, Richard had surprised Ann with a flat, point-blank refusal of children. He had continued to lie to her family and friends about *everything*. He had refused to take care of his health. His depression worsened. His cotton candy, diabetic breath in her face each night had been sweet and comforting at times. Other times, Ann had shivered at the thought of the pounds of sugar Richard poured down his neck in her absence. In her mind, Ann had watched the huge rock candy chunks bouncing through his broken-down veins, cutting and scraping as they went along. Richard's self-loathing and bitterness had replaced laughter and love like bands of pus-filled shingles across a back that refused to heal. Bursting. Bursting. Bursting.

"I won't stand by and watch you kill yourself. You're committing feckin' suicide. I won't be part of it."

"You don't have to. I'm already gone."

In the end, no measure of soothing-tea relationship poultices or mouth-to-mouth, soul-saving measures could be applied. Ann couldn't save the relationship. Ann couldn't save Richard. She had decided to save *herself*.

Not long before Katie's first email, Richard had called out of the blue and dumped angry words on Ann's doorstep—unloading infinite bags of stinking, rotting rubbish, one-by-one.

"You're selfish. All you care about is YOU. Stop sending me cards. Stop checking on me. Stop calling me. Stop texting me. You're bad for me. I can take care of myself. I don't want to talk to you anymore. *I* am done with *you*. IT'S POINTLESS!"

Ann's hurt and anger over all that had happened had finally gotten the best of her. Instead of calling Richard back and completely losing control, she had flown over to the computer. She couldn't bear to hear his voice. As if she were a swishy pink genie in a bottle, "WISH GRANTED!" Ann had tapped on the keyboard with one hard finger like she was hammering coffin nails in for good.

On sleepless nights, Ann couldn't keep herself from stalking Katie online. Without being a "friend," she could only see so much on Katie's private Facebook page. Ann noticed Katie had recently joined every manner of sale groups possible in her area—"Cars for Sale," "Books for Sale," "Unique Gifts for Sale." Ann swallowed down buckets of choking tears when she spied Katie's post on one of the many "Books for Sale or Swap" groups.

There it was, in the middle of a tall, leaning stack of Stephen King books in someone's filthy living room—*Hearts in Atlantis*. Ann covered her eyes with both hands and moaned.

Ann could see Richard's face when she handed him the signed copy of *Hearts in Atlantis* for his birthday. She had thought the massive truck driver might actually cry. The crepey wrinkles around Richard's twinkling blue eyes had sunk deeper into his face, vanishing almost entirely. Richard had flown around the house, picking things up and putting them down again like a nervous granny. He had recited eloquent lines from the book in the shower as if he were Stephen King himself doing a prepared reading for an excited audience of thousands. He had smiled all day, even in his sleep. It was the first book Richard had read to Ann over the phone before drifting off each night. Long, sleepy hours spent listening to Richard's deep voice stringing descriptive words together were burned forever into Ann's brain. *Hearts in Atlantis* had come up in almost every conversation like some weird King version of *Six Degrees of Kevin Bacon*.

A dollar? A DOLLAR.

Did Richard's niece think that the signed first edition and best-birthday-present-ever *Hearts in Atlantis* was worth only a *dollar*?

Apparently, she did.

"He's gone now. *Things* don't matter," Ann said to herself in her empty living room.

Ann moved from the computer chair to the sofa and back again. She was finding it hard to breathe. Her heart raced. She pounded her chest with her fist harder than expected, leaving a red mark that lasted for hours.

"Our memories are worth A DOLLAR," Ann said to no one.

Bloody fury floated in a raging river behind Ann's closed, throbbing eyes.

Suddenly, Richard's smiling face appeared. He placed a big-lipped kiss on top of Ann's head, making a dramatic smooching noise as he did. With her eyes still closed, Ann felt the sides of her mouth pulling up into a reluctant, tired smile. Beaming, Richard held *Hearts in Atlantis* high, high in the air with his heavily-tattooed arm. He proclaimed regally in his favorite fake British accent, "BEST. GIFT. EVA!"

***

Martin polished off the last of the butter pecan. He shoveled heaping spoonfuls into his already-full mouth. He had perused the signed copy of *Hearts in Atlantis* a few times now. It still hadn't lost its thrill. It probably never would.

Martin turned to page 192 randomly. An old photo stuck between the pages tumbled out onto his lap. Martin looked at the photo with just the tiniest ounce of fleeting interest. Some old, bald, fat guy with a much younger blonde girl hugging his thick neck. Both smiling. *Huh. Wonder how he got her. Good job, Old Fat Guy.* Martin turned the photo over and squinted his eyes to read the writing without his glasses.

"Hearts can break. Yes, hearts can break. Sometimes I think it would be better if we died when they did, but we don't."

Martin turned the photo over once more in his hands and looked briefly at the happy couple again.

Martin shouldn't have paid that bookseller one hundred dollars for *Hearts in Atlantis*. Although, it was actually worth way more, and they both knew it. The bookseller might just be sweet on him. This proved it. She was SO weird. She was a loner because she was just plain strange. She was most definitely a serious hoarder. She liked to argue all the time. She could get on a person's nerves within mere seconds. Totally set in her ways. Irritating. Odd. Who would ever date her?

Maybe Martin would take her to the *All You Can Eat Mandarin Gourmet Buffet* next week.

Martin sighed. He laid *Hearts in Atlantis* on the edge of his chair. He carried the empty butter pecan container to the overflowing trashcan and smashed it down with two hands. Without looking—or giving it another thought—Martin aimlessly tossed the couple's photo on top of the heap. He heroically flung the smelly trash bag into the old creaky dumpster and slammed the cracked lid shut with a loud bang .

Coming Soon from Dawn A. Fuller
Tuomb Beoir (A Good Woman)

Meet the *Beoirs*.

Embark upon a compelling journey alongside twelve marginalized women from Ireland—*Irish Travellers*—as they make their brave way down country roads of untold beauty and heartbreaking tragedy. The gutsy *Traveller Beoirs* will have you laughing and crying as they reveal their secret, courageous struggles to love their stalwart men, ferociously protect their spirited children, unpack their rich heritage, and let their proud, strong voices *finally* be heard loud and clear. In *Tuomb Beoir*, you are an invited guest of the unapologetic pioneer *Beoirs* as they shamelessly unveil themselves in all their glory to the insular world of the *Settled*.

Excerpt from *Tuomb Beoir (A Good Woman)*
Ghostes

Do you believe in ghostes?

I do.

I am not here, but I *am* here.

How long is it before someone forgets you after you're dead? A
month? A year? Three years? Five? Ten?

How long before the sharp mental photograph of you tacked up on
the picture walls of their minds starts fading and blurring? How long
until the ruby reds, crisp greens, sunny yellows, and candy pinks of
who you once were start to change shape—slowly-but-surely—into
poorly-erased pencil drawings?

I have been thinking about that a lot lately.

I wonder if they forget you straight away. I never forgot anyone I
ever lost—a good Traveller Beoir wouldn't. I celebrated their birthdays,
weddings, anniversaries, death days, and more—long after they were
gone—just the same as if they were still there. I was always tending to
my ones' graves. I said my rosary over and over for them. I lit tall holy
candles and watched their crooked wicks bend and flicker this way and
that, floating down into low, sweet pools of melted wax. I prayed to
wee Saint Anthony for their souls. I kept the dead in my heart. I never
forgot. I never would.

I believe in ghostes. I do.

I have heard people here say it takes time to work out that you
have actually died. Some linger too long trying to figure that part out—
thinking they're still alive, or refusing to accept that they've long since
moved on. They are absolute *miseries* I can tell you. When we pass each

other along the way, I try to have a friendly wee chat. They aren't having it. No, all they do is whinge about how none of their living ones can see or hear them. "Not fair, not *fair*," they say. They remind me of boring auld fashioned ghostes I used to see in the films—always hanging about cobwebby houses with broken windows all spooky-like, tangled up in rusty chains and crinkled bed sheets with black, sunken eyes. Howly, howly all the time. In the end, all they do is scare the daylights out of the only ones who can actually see them when it's turned midnight—the little children alone in the dark, with their mudders and fadders sleeping away in the next room.

Yes, those ones are miseries. They can bring you right down if you let them. I never had it easy in life. Things weren't "fair," but I got on with it. I am getting on with it now. Have to.

Things were different than I imagined they would be. I *did* see a light. It wasn't the light you think of, though. It wasn't a comforting light at the end of a long tunnel the priests say you'll see when you cross over to your new home with Jesus, Mary, Joseph, and all of the angels and saints.

Mine was a fire light. It was the foul, smothering light of the divil himself. With his wicked forked tongue, he licked up every single thing I ever loved.

I can just shiver when I think of it.

My body is the same. It's not really a "new body" you hear about. It's still the same auld one I had after the babies. I have to say, it does feel a little firmer now. Bernie would like that, so he would. It's light and lovely. I don't even pay attention to it most of the time. No need for it.

Time is mine own. I go where I want. I do what I want. Some days, I go back to see my mudder and fadder, brudders and sisters. When Bernie and I got married and moved away, I missed them desperately. My heart was broke. Now, I can see them as much as I want. It's nice most of the time. Sometimes, it isn't. My mudder cries and cries. My fadder tries to comfort her. At night's end, he almost always falls asleep in his battered recliner with a tall whiskey tipping over his full belly and a salty tear sitting fat and thick on his red cheek.

My brudders and sisters are bad cases too. They have to carry on, if not for their own sakes, then for their husbands', wives', and children's, don't they? I like to watch my brudders and sisters—working, dancing, messing, loving, fighting, or even eating and sleeping. *Living.* I love being near them. Makes me remember the good auld days. I sit next to them—crying and laughing out loud like I am still really there. Like I am finally *home.*

When I feel up to it, I go back to the Old Killcreavy Road Halting Site. It was the first place I went after. I tried to work everything out in my mind then, get everything straight. There was still thick, grey smoke rising up—step-by-step—on a rickety stepladder straight to heaven. It floated up, up, up from the warped mobile home for a long time. Ashy embers popped and glowed for days—from orange, to red, to black, to grey, to white, and back to orange again—when the wind whipped down the hill like Fionn mac Cumhaill's giant hand swiping down, toppling everything I had ever known and loved.

I saw what was left of the tiny, sunken bed where Bernie and I had slept and loved—where we explored each other's young bodies, learning every soft groove and rounded curve; the second-hand bed where we made our fine, handsome boys under the colorful blanket my mudder sewed for our wedding day. I can hear my husband Bernie whispering warm against my cool ear, "Bridget, my beautiful Bridget, my *Tuomb Beoir,*" while he loved me, and I loved him.

My *husband.* I still like to say it.

I saw the children's favorite toys scattered carelessly around the site—a flattened footie ball, a disfigured yellow digger with three wheels covered in black ash, melted boxing gloves, and the fancy bike wee Francis loved to ride. That bike was the cause of many a fight between Francis and his younger brudder, Michael. It makes me smile. They had each other kilt. Now, the bike lay silently in the sizzling dirt—a misshapen, melty skeleton. Bernie could have sold it for scrap. Would have got him a pound or two. Ha! Would you listen to me?

If you took away the burned-up look of it all, you could almost pretend that the children heard me shout down for dinner. You could picture them throwing everything down mid-play and running toward the mobile home with rumbling bellies and the rich smell of hot coddle running up their perfect little noses. If you ignored it *all*—especially the wailing people standing 'round the site with their swollen eyes, worry-worn hands covering their mouths in shock—you could imagine we'd abandoned everything in a mad rush. You could dream that we'd run off to a faraway land from the fairy stories to nibble sugary fruit off leafy trees, float all day long on our backs in the glittery sea, and sleep together forever under the happy sun.

Do you believe in ghostes?

I do.

I am here.

I am here.

I am *here*.

Dear Sweet, Merciful God, I AM HERE.

About the Author

 Dawn A. Fuller is a Hungarian-American writer who grew up in the desolate, desperately hot, and nearly-forgotten Imperial Valley. She lives in Pasadena, California. When she isn't writing, she enjoys shameless hours book collecting and spending time with her best friends—her mom and dad. Dawn's work has been featured in Adanna Literary Journal, Black Fox Literary Journal, Boyne Berries, and more. She is completing her first novel, *Tuomb Beoir*, due out in 2019.

52757899R00023

Made in the USA
San Bernardino, CA
28 August 2017